For all refugees and those who help them
—AB

For SB
—SU

Little, Brown and Company

Hachette Book Group
1290 Avenue of the Americas, New York, NY 10104
Visit us at lb-kids.com

Little, Brown and Company is a division of Hachette Book Group, Inc.
The Little, Brown name and logo are trademarks of Hachette Book Group, Inc.

The publisher is not responsible for websites (or their content) that are not owned by the publisher.

First US Edition: October 2016
Originally published in the UK in 2015 by Nosy Crow Ltd.

ISBN 978-0-316-36172-9

10 9 8 7 6 5 4 3 2 1

IM

PRINTED IN CHINA

Refuge

Anne Booth & Sam Usher

L B

LITTLE, BROWN AND COMPANY
New York   Boston

The man led me, and I carried the woman all the way to Bethlehem . . .

And then the baby was born.

The shepherds came first . . .

And after them
came the kings . . .

When the last king left, the scent of
frankincense lingering in the air, we all
slept and the man had a dream.

   A dream of danger.

He woke long before the sun rose and told
the woman. She took the baby and kissed him.
She smelled his sweet baby breath, and felt his soft,
warm baby skin and how his lashes tickled her
cheek as he sleepily nuzzled her neck.

"Time to go," she said.

Then they wrapped him up warm and kissed him again, and the man came to get me. He patted me between the ears and led me out.

"Come on, old friend, we're off on a journey again."
And we left some gold for the innkeeper,
for he had been good to us, when others had not.

And we set off . . .

. . . under starlight, through empty streets,

And I kept walking, carrying my precious load,

and the woman held the baby close to her heart,

and she and the man talked, about journeys,

and dreams and warnings,

and the love of a baby,

and the kindness of strangers.

And when we rested,
and they were frightened,
they took hope from each other,
and from the baby's tiny first smile.

And we entered into Egypt . . .

. . . and we found refuge.